"Neil guides us on a trip through life's emotions... the gift of love available to each of us when we open and surrender in our worst fears and realise the gift therein. Read this and be inspired."

Brandon Bays
International Bestselling Author of The Journey

"A beautiful allegory for our times of the seasons of our lives, of re-empowerment, and what it really means to be alive. This is a story to share with those you love."

Jonathan Horwitz
Co-Director of the Scandinavian Centre for Shamanic Studies

"Beautifully enriching and glittering....soul awakening."

Jimena Paratcha Page
President of the ABC Trust

"This book is astounding! I could not put it down, it is simply so pure and beautiful and heart opening!"

Cate Mackenzie
International Workshop Leader and Coach

The Flower in
the Desert

Neil del Strother

To order a copy of this book visit:
www.theflowerinthedesert.com

A kindle version of this book can be downloaded from
www.amazon.co.uk An ibook is also available. Both are
designed by www.Wiredthing.com

Second edition 2011; Third edition 2012; Fourth edition
2013; Fifth edition 2014; Sixth edition 2015

ISBN 978-0-9563471-3-8

The Flower in the Desert is also published in Italy, by
Overview Editore; translated by Luigina Malvestio.

Cover designed by Lorna Holdcroft
www.lornaholdcroft.co.uk

For Isola

A man can love another more than himself

"There are always flowers for those who want to see them"

Henri Matisse

1

Sati lived alone, in a small hut on the edge of the village on the edge of the great desert. Living alone was unheard of for such a young boy, but Sati wanted it that way and no-one, however hard they tried, could persuade him to do otherwise.

His mother had died first. In childbirth, taking the unborn brother he'd longed for with her. He'd lived with his father after that, just the two of them. His father did his best for the seven year old boy, but the simple truth was he hadn't the will to live on without his beloved wife.

One terrible morning, three years to the day after his wife died, in the middle of the marketplace, Sati's father died too. Of a heart attack they said, but even at such a tender age Sati knew his father had died of a broken heart.

After that, many of Sati's relatives and neighbours insisted he come and live with them in their homes. He thanked them all very politely, but he refused to move from the home he'd shared with the mother and father he'd loved so much.

His hut wasn't much to look at, just a one-room dusty shack, but in it was held the tender kiss of his mother and the shy smile of his father. In it was held his childhood.

By the time he was 13 years old Sati was grown up in all but years. Unlike the other children in the village he didn't go to school. Instead he scratched a living looking after two woebegone camels that his neighbour Mushta used for taking tourists out for trips into the desert.

This work did not generate much of an income as the village attracted few tourists, but even so Mushta guarded his business closely and with immense suspicion. He was the only man in the village who took tourists into the desert and he was fearful of competition – not least from Sati, who he feared would set up on his own when he was a little older.

"You are not to be trusted," he said one day to Sati with a dismissive flick of his hand. All Sati had done was tie a saddle just a bit too loose. Not enough to be a danger, but it was more than enough to bring on Mushta's anger.

Sati cried that night. Quietly, alone, in the silent darkness of his home – just as he had when first his mother, and then his father, had died. He knew very well what it was not to trust. His

3

parents taken from him, he did not trust life. Now he was not to be trusted himself.

Sati worked even harder than before, with a desperate intensity, to prove Mushta wrong, to prove himself wrong, to prove the world wrong. He worked even longer hours, tending the camels from the first break of light in the morning until it faded into the soft nothingness of evening. He made no more mistakes and the camels thrived like never before, becoming lustrous and healthy.

Slowly, very slowly, Mushta began to soften. He was not without feeling. He too had once been a child and he too had known the lonely ache of an absent father. His father had left for months on end each year, travelling on his camel to trade in far off lands. Mushta rarely thought of it now, but deep down his body still held a desperate longing.

One evening Mushta came to Sati as he was brushing the camels. "I have been watching you these past months and you have worked well – day in and day out," he said, his face stern. He paused before breaking into a smile. "When the next tourists come you can help me lead them out into the desert."

A great joy rose in Sati's heart and he too had an urge to smile. But he had learned a long time ago that a smile could be dangerous; that a smile brought loss. "Thank you master," he replied solemnly, with just the slightest nod of his head.

That night, alone in his home, Sati cried once again. Tears of joy, mixed with tears of sorrow for two people who would never hear of his success.

2

Days slowly drifted into weeks and no tourists came. Sati was disappointed, but not surprised. At most, only two or three tourists came to the village each month. And even when they came they often left quickly again; too quickly at least to take a trip into the desert.

Not everyone fell under the spell of the lonely village, with its one dark shop and its humble huddled huts. Not everyone wanted to go on a camel trip. It was hot and uncomfortable and it meant tumbling from the safe arms of the village into the vast nothingness of the desert.

Eventually though some tourists did come, as Sati knew they would. Two men from a country far away who wanted to spend a night out in the desert. Their eyes were bright with that fire-full excitement that, once ignited, is never extinguished.

Mushta knocked at Sati's door at five o'clock the next morning: "We are going into the desert – go and get the camels ready," he said simply and turned on his heel.

Sati was up in less than a minute.

They did not travel very far, only a few miles, but even so the village was completely engulfed within the desert sands. In the darkness of the night they could have been a million miles from anywhere.

Sati had never ventured so far away from his home before. This was unusual in the village. Most boys of thirteen years had travelled into the desert. It was the tradition for fathers to take their sons there on their twelfth birthdays, walking without camels for three days deep into the sands, as an initiation into young adulthood.

Sati had watched so many of the other boys leave the village with their fathers; with a longing he couldn't fully understand as they slowly disappeared into the sand and rock. He knew it was not for him; that it would never be for him.

But now, with Mushta and the tourists, he was leading a camel where he would have walked with his father. He thought of his father's rough chin and his warm eyes, crinkled in the sun. He felt his father's hand on his shoulder and heard, in the dry breeze, his father's blessing. Sati turned his head so no one would see the damp in his eyes.

They walked from dawn to dusk before setting up camp among some low sand dunes. Sati did not speak. He hardly noticed the tourists and he hardly heard a word that Mushta said to them about the desert.

Mushta said very little to him other than to bark an occasional instruction. Sati walked in silence, alone with his thoughts, his hand loose on the tether of the smaller of the two camels. He gazed unseeingly into the heart of the desert, away from where the village lay.

3

Sati now travelled into the desert with Mushta whenever tourists came. And in the long days and weeks between their coming he tended to the camels exactly as he had done before.

Mushta treated him with growing kindness. He no longer barked orders and, when he was given a tip by the tourists, he shared it half and half with him. Sometimes when they were back in the village he would bring food, cooked by his wife, to Sati's hut and eat it with him cross-legged on the rough floor.

Sati rarely visited Mushta's house. He was welcome, but he did not like to go. It reminded

him too much of what he did not have; of what
had been lost. On the rare occasions he did go
he was treated with great kindness by Mushta's
wife Meera. She welcomed him like a prince
and plied him with soft and sugary sweets from
the big glass jar that sat on a rickety shelf above
her fireplace.

Sati often spent time with Fellima, the second
of Mushta's three daughters, who was three years
younger than him. Most days she came to the
well and chatted to him when he went to collect
water for the camels. Sometimes she would visit
him when he was tending to the camels and help
him brush their coats. She was the nearest thing
he had to a friend.

Sati grew with the years; not tall, but taller.
He was a slight figure for a fifteen year old boy,

with fine features and his father's kindly eye. He walked with grace and softness. He did not smile.

One baking afternoon, when he and Mushta were taking some tourists, a newly wedded couple, out into the desert, Sati noticed that Mushta was not leading his camel with quite his usual ease. He was stopping more often than usual to chat to the tourists, taking more rests while he smilingly told them some of the great tales of the desert.

Sati could see his smile hid pain. He said nothing, but as the weeks passed he noticed that Mushta was stopping more and more often to rest on their trips and that he wasn't taking the tourists quite as far into the desert as he had before.

Early one morning, as they were saddling the camels together, Sati saw a quick grimace of pain pass across Mushta's face. He could hold back no longer. "Master, what is wrong?" he asked.

Mushta glared sharply at him with angry eyes. But not for long; soon they filled with a softness of tears that would not be shed. "I do not know," he replied quietly. "But I no longer feel the youth in my body and my heart is heavy." He shook his head. "I do not know," he said again.

Sati heard the distance in his voice and asked nothing more.

4

Sati watched Mushta's decline in silence, in a depth of sadness that had no words. He was all too familiar with death, but he had not witnessed the agony of a slow death before.

For a while Mushta still came out with him and the tourists into the desert. But before long he chose to stay at home. He did not speak about it; he gave no explanations or excuses. He only asked Sati to: "treat the camels and the tourists well."

Sati did as he was asked, and when he returned from the desert trips he always brought whatever money he had made and any tip he'd been given to Mushta.

Mushta always gave him half the money back, kissing it in thanks and blessing it as he handed it over. Each time he would smile and say: "thank you, you are a good boy". At this Sati's eyes crinkled like his father's had before him, but a smile never quite met his lips.

The day of Mushta's death came. He was lying in his bed when Sati arrived, Meera and his three daughters sitting by his side. He raised his head weakly to look at Sati with faraway eyes. "I am leaving you now, my son," he said, his voice a whisper.

Sati's legs felt weak. He held onto the bed to stop himself falling. He wanted to scream no, to deny the words, but he knew this was a lie. He looked at Mushta, his eyes like thick morning mist.

Mushta looked into a distance that Sati couldn't see. "I am leaving, and soon I will meet our God," he said. He paused for a long moment with the effort of speaking and looked at Sati. He gazed deep into his eyes. "I have something to ask of you; that you continue to run our business as before; that you look after our camels and take the tourists into the desert as we have done for so long together – and that you give a little of the money you make to my wife and daughters so that they will not suffer too much with my leaving."

The words would not come, but Sati did not need to speak. He nodded his head, almost imperceptibly.

"I always knew I could trust you," said Mushta with just the hint of a smile; his voice so soft it was almost a breath. His eyes closed for the last time.

5

The tourists still did not come all that often to the village, and even fewer wanted to travel out into the desert, but when they did Sati treated them as honoured guests, learning and using words and phrases from many of their languages to put them at their ease.

After each trip he brought all the money that he made and any tips he was given to Meera. And always she would give him half the money back, kissing it in thanks and blessing it as she handed it to him.

Sati enjoyed these visits. Even though he deeply grieved the loss of Mushta, he no longer felt the sadness of coming to his house that he'd felt before. In its place he felt an excitement, an exquisite longing. Fellima was fifteen now. She was no longer the little girl who had come to chat with him by the well and who had sometimes helped him to brush the camels.

Sati felt awkward and nervous when Fellima was around. Although she was three years younger than him he thought of her as older, more knowing. He didn't dare speak to her, he couldn't find any words, but sometimes she would look at him, a quick glance with her dark eyes, and he would shudder inside.

6

It was the hottest month and Sati knew that no tourists would come. This was the quietest time in the village, when the heat was so intense there was little to be done but sit and rest in the shade.

Sati stayed mainly in his hut, only venturing out early in the morning and evening to tend to his camels.

One night, when the heat left him uneasy in his bed, he had a dream. He dreamt of a vast nothingness – endless, empty and yet so full that it felt ready to burst. He awoke and looked out of his window. The desert had called to him.

Sati put all the money he'd saved in an earthenware jar with a note saying that if he didn't come back it was for Meera and her daughters, and placed it carefully on a shelf in a dark corner of his hut. Then he packed a large bag full of dry fruit to eat on the journey and walked out of his door into the scorching heat.

He saddled up his favourite camel and filled a large sack full of food for it for the journey and attached it to its saddle. Then he checked there was enough water in the trough for the camel he was leaving behind and enough food in the manger for it to eat while he was away.

Once he'd finished, Sati hauled himself up into the saddle of his favourite camel and rode to the well. He dismounted and filled two large carriers with water and waited while his camel drank its fill.

Everyone was inside sheltering from the sun, so no one saw him leave the village gates. No one that is, except for one young girl. Her dark flashing eyes gazed intently after him from the darkness of her hut as he disappeared into the endless desert.

Sati did not follow his normal route, the route he took the tourists. Instead he headed due east, directly towards the heart of the desert. He felt no fear, just a deep knowing, a certainty that he didn't understand.

It did not take long for the terrain to become unfamiliar. The stones, the sands, the hidden valleys he knew so well soon turned into a more barren, more vast landscape of endless flatness. Here and there the monotony was interspersed by awkward and lonely rocks, so large and solitary Sati wondered if they'd fallen from the skies.

The sand underfoot changed too. It became more uncertain and it shifted and gave way unexpectedly under his camel's spread toes. The camel walked tentatively, feeling its way with each large flat foot, testing each step before walking on.

They travelled across this desolate and baking wasteland for three days. Each night Sati slept next to his camel, connected by a heartbeat, under the stars, under a sky so vast that Sati felt lost in nothingness. Each morning he awoke full of a desire to go home, but somehow driven to travel further into the heart of the desert.

On the afternoon of the fourth day the desert changed. The flatness gave way to great sweeping sand dunes, monstrous waves in a raging yellow sea. Sati steered his camel through the dark valleys between these fearsome dunes, fearful lest he be engulfed by one crashing down over his head.

Two nights they slept beneath the vast dunes, hidden and unseen in their dry depths. The following morning they emerged from their shadow into an area of longer lower rolling dunes, beautiful and sure underfoot. Sati drove his camel straight up and over their stretched slopes and was rewarded at each soft peak with breathtaking views of the undulating desert.

Sati did not stop long to admire the views. He felt a greater urgency. He only had enough water and food to allow him to ride for another two days before having to turn back towards the village.

He rode onwards, directly towards the morning sun, never waning, full of a certainty and knowing that he did not understand. As he rode he thought about all the days, months and years he'd spent alone, and of the years he'd spent with his father and the death of his father, and of the years he'd spent with his mother and the death of his mother.

Tears that had been hidden in his heart, far beneath the tears he already knew too well, smarted in his eyes. He cried and cried, deep in the desert, alone.

With his eyes glazed and unseeing, Sati dismounted from his camel. He walked cautiously forwards, leading his camel by its tether. Perhaps an hour passed like this, perhaps a day, perhaps only a few minutes. No time. All that Sati knew was that a moment arrived when his camel came to a quiet stop and would walk no further.

He wiped his eyes and looked around. He could see no reason why his camel had come to a halt. There was nothing remarkable about the desert in front and about him. Perhaps the sand looked somehow finer and more even than it had before, but Sati thought this was probably his imagination.

He was just about to pull his camel forward once again when he saw it – no more than two or three feet in front of him, snug within a little dip in the sand. Growing straight from the dryness was a single beautiful flower. Its small bloom vivid yellow, a gorgeous sun in the heart of the desert.

He sat down next to the flower and touched it delicately with his fingers. If felt soft and full. In his heart he felt a joy, unbidden, a freedom. He knew why he had travelled so deep into the desert.

Sati sat with the flower through the night, silent, not sleeping, hardly moving, just still. When the sun was high again in the sky he knew it was time to leave. Touching the flower delicately one last time he mounted his camel and rode off towards the west. He did not look back.

Not long into his journey home he felt a quickening in his body. A pressure building deep inside, something blocked, like a river stuck and swelling behind a dam. He pushed it away, but it grew and grew. And then it burst.

Sati's body shook and twisted like it was possessed, writhing from side to side, his head lurching forwards and backwards and his mind flooded with a fear beyond anything he had ever known. He fought desperately for calmness, trying to hold himself still, but the force of the fear was too much. He fell from his camel and landed hard on his back, knocked unconscious.

He came to in a soft orange desert, the sun low in the sky. He felt utterly exhausted and beaten and battered, and empty, so empty, as if all he had ever been had been violently sucked and pulled out from within him. He felt a terrible loss and desolation.

He stood up unsteadily and hobbled over to his nearby camel. He mounted it gingerly, his face a grimace of pain, and rode off once again into the west.

7

Sati arrived back at his village in the clear bright starlight of desert evening. Meera was there at the village gates to meet him. "My son, where have you been? Are you all right? You've been gone so long. What came over you? We thought you were dead," she said, her voice a mix of relief and anger.

Sati was quiet. Fond though he was of Meera, he could find nothing to say. He did not want to speak of the flower and, in particular, he did not want to speak of the terrible fear. He wanted to force it from his mind.

A voice, as soft as a young child's laugh, flowed into his quietness. "I knew you were alive," it said.

"I have always known."

Sati looked up in shy surprise. Fellima was standing in the shadow by the side of the gate. She was searching him with her dark flashing eyes. They were full of an openness and trust that he realised, in that moment, he had spent his whole life longing for.

Sati did not resist when Meera asked him to come to dinner after he'd fed and watered his camel. And he certainly did not resist when, after dinner, she said she had to go out for a few minutes – with her two other daughters, Fellima's sisters – to borrow some flour from a neighbour to make bread for the morning.

Sati sat alone with Fellima. Tongue-tied, he said more or less nothing, but by the time Meera and her other daughters returned with a bag full of flour, the date was set. Sati had never been so happy.

They married two weeks later. Fellima had always known it would be so. Sati, being a man, and at 19 years old he was now very much a man, had not had the slightest inkling.

8

Sati and Fellima had a daughter, a beautiful girl they called Mushtina, in honour of her grandfather. They tried for more children over the years, but none came. Fellima felt it was her fault and one day took the courage to say as much to Sati.

Sati longed for a son, but he knew now that this gift would not be given him. He looked deep into Fellima's eyes. "What God has seen fit to give us is a gift more precious than I could ever have imagined," he said. He felt at peace. He loved his daughter more than his own life. He put his arms around Fellima. She knew he meant every word.

Sati and his small family lived well. More tourists now came to the village and Sati took them into the desert most weeks, bringing him a healthy income. He loved his job. In particular, he enjoyed hearing about the many places around the world the tourists came from.

He sometimes thought about the flower he'd found in the heart of the desert. And each time he thought of it he felt again, just for a moment, the joy and peace he'd felt sitting by its side. But then, in a rush, he felt again the terrible fear that had consumed him after he left the flower. He feared this fear beyond anything.

So Sati did his utmost to push any thoughts of the flower away. He never told anyone of the flower, of where he'd been on his long journey, of the joy and the fear, not even Fellima. And if she wondered at all, she never asked.

As time passed he thought less and less about the flower. But sometimes it would appear as a quiet thought in a moment of stillness. And each time this short peace was followed, unbidden, by the desperate fear.

9

One morning, when Mushtina was fully thirteen years old, she came to Sati as he was feeding his camels – he now had seven. "Father, can I speak with you?" she asked, her words hushed.

It was a voice Sati did not recognise. Inside he felt a quickening, an echo from the past. And although he didn't want to, he nodded for Mushtina to go on.

"Last night I had a dream, a terrible dream, one like I've never had before," she continued nervously. "I dreamt of you. You were on your favourite camel, in a vast emptiness, all alone. You were very scared, but you kept going further into this nothingness, further and further. Eventually you…"

Sati raised his hand to stop her. He paused, the world still. "This nothingness," he asked at last. "What did it look like?"

"It was a place of endless space, of sand and rock."

Sati nodded. He knew this place only too well.

Mushtina continued. "Eventually you reached an area that felt different to where you'd been, although it looked no different at all. It felt safer somehow, more calm. You sat there, leaving your camel to wander. And then….and then….," she hesitated, tears racing to her eyes. "And then you died and your body rotted away," she sobbed, trying to hold it all back. "You rotted away before my eyes. And once you'd gone all that was left was a small flower."

The two of them were quiet for a long time. The only sound was Mushtina's muted sobs.

"Was it a yellow flower?" asked Sati at last.

"Like a small sun."

Sati nodded. And in his eyes Mushtina saw a strangeness, something unfamiliar, something she had never seen there before.

Sati felt a deep weariness, a melancholy. "It is time," he said quietly. "I can hide no more."

The next morning Sati told Fellima, in a calm and matter of fact voice, that he had to leave for ten days or even more, and that during that time any tourists who wanted to be taken out into the desert would have to be turned away.

Fellima heard the fear under his calmness. Her heart beat with an urgency of concern, but she loved Sati as much as she loved herself and she only replied: "My darling I am waiting for you to return. Go with God."

Sati took food and water for a long trip. Mounting his favourite camel, he waved a quick goodbye to Fellima and Mushtina and rode off into the vastness of the desert. He didn't look back.

He rode straight, without deviation, not thinking, remembering the route he'd taken so many years before. In many places the sand had shifted and the landscape seemed unfamiliar, but even there he somehow knew where to go. His being knew.

A quickening rose slowly in him as he travelled deeper and deeper into the desert. Each step his camel took felt heavier than the last. He did not want to go any further. He thought of his wife and his daughter and he wondered if he would ever see them again. He drove his camel forward into the vastness.

On the third night a huge wind came, stirring the sand into a frenzy. It bit and stung Sati viciously as he rode. He dismounted and huddled with his camel in a small ravine, covering his head with his scarf.

The wind blew all through the day and all through the night. It finally abated as the sun rose once again. Sati pulled and pushed himself and his camel out of the heavy sand that had almost completely buried them. Puffing heavily with the effort he gazed around at the desert. It looked different, as if it was new. For a moment he felt a panic, unsure of where he was and where he had to go. Clarity came on his next breath. He knew.

Sati rode for five days and five nights; only stopping for an hour here and there to rest his camel and to grab a few minutes fitful sleep.

All the time he rode he questioned what he was doing, wondered about its wisdom and worried about what might happen to him all alone in the emptiness.

He wanted to turn back and to fall back into the loving arms of Fellima and Mushtina. On more than one occasion he turned his camel, but then he remembered Mushtina's dream and he knew there was no choice. The flower was calling to him.

At last Sati neared the centre of the desert, the place he'd so often remembered and so often driven from his mind.

He stopped his camel and dismounted. Around him he could see nothing but sand, stretching into the horizon. He searched the sand in front of him. His heart beat quickly. He hoped the flower had gone. He hoped that it was no more.

He gasped. No longer one flower but two. So beautiful, in a small dip in the sand, no more than two or three feet in front of him. Two delicate yellow suns hidden in the eternity of the desert.

He sat down by the flowers, in silence. He felt calm. He thought of his wife and his daughter, and of his mother and his father, and tears of gratitude and joy gurgled and bubbled up to him from deep in the earth, like pure water to a fountain.

Sati stayed with the flowers, fully awake, through the night. As the moments passed he slowed to a stillness, to a nothingness. From time to time a thought or a feeling came and he allowed it to come, not resisting, letting it do what it wanted to do, letting it go where it wanted to go, and letting it drift away again.

Not long after Sati left the flowers the fear he had dreaded for so many years came once again, a torrent, like water flooding from a crumbling dam, racking his body and twisting and turning him with its force, threatening to throw him from his camel.

But this time he did not resist the fear. He did not fight it. This time he allowed a death.

How long the fear lasted he did not know. He had no sense of time. All he knew was that it left as suddenly as it had come, leaving him exhausted and empty.

He sat quietly for some time before riding on. And with each step of his camel he felt the slow rising of a peace; a silent dawn rising from the west. He felt something lifted within him; something he'd never even known was there. By the time he approached his village he was full of joy.

Fellima and Mushtina ran out to greet him. "Thank God you are back safely," said Fellima quietly, her eyes full of tears, her voice full of love.

Mushtina said nothing. But Sati saw the joy in her eyes, love that was a mirror to the endless sky. He smiled, just the slightest smile, a first smile, and a thousand million stars shivered in the heavens.

10

Sati said nothing at all, not a word. But even in his quietness Fellima and Mushtina saw the change in him. His eyes shone bright and his skin, his whole being, seemed somehow more alive than before.

They did not speak to him. They did not ask him where he had travelled. It was for Sati to speak and for him to tell of where he'd been when he was ready. This was the tradition in the village.

And so it was when his words started to flow once again. They did not ask. They allowed him to gently slip back into the life he had led before – almost the same, but somehow changed.

Weeks and months passed and more and more tourists visited the village, and more and more of them took camel trips out into the desert. After each trip, as he had always done, Sati gave the money he'd earned to Meera. And she gave half of it back to him, kissing and blessing it, as she had always done.

Meera was now old and her needs were few, so she kept even less of the money for herself than before. She gave most of it to her two other daughters, who both had growing families of their own.

Sati felt at peace. One evening, sitting quietly outside his hut with Fellima and Mushtina, he realised that he was truly happy. He felt the soft caress of a thousand blessings. His eyes moistened with a mixture of joy for what is and sadness for what has passed.

Fellima looked into his eyes. "What is it?" she asked tenderly.

Sati looked at her for a long moment, and then at Mushtina. In them he found his strength. "I have a story to tell you," he began.

He told them about his first trip into the desert so many years before, of his dream and his time with the flower – and of the terrible fear that had thrown him from his camel. He told them of the many years of hiding from it all and the effort of trying to forget. Then he told them of his recent trip, of how Mushtina's dream, like his own dream so many years before, had left him with no choice but to go. And he told them of the two flowers.

When he finished Mushtina stuck out her chin. "Next time you go we're coming too," she said stubbornly.

At the hottest time of the year, the time when no tourists came to the village, Sati set out into the desert once again. He travelled with three camels: one for him, one for Fellima and one for Mushtina.

The journey was even easier this time. Sati was surer of the way and the company of Fellima and Mushtina helped time pass more quickly. The quiet fears he'd harboured that they might find the journey too arduous were quickly dispelled. They chatted and laughed and were completely at ease riding across the nothingness of sand and rock.

After five days they approached the heart of the desert. Even though Sati was looking out for them Mushtina saw them first. "Look – how beautiful," she screamed with joy, jumping from her camel and rushing towards the flowers.

Fellima looked at Sati. "But you said there were two," she said in surprise.

Four beautiful flowers, as yellow as the sun, were growing in a tight bunch, filling a small dip in the sand. Sati smiled, as proud as a new father There was no need for words.

The three of them sat down next to the flowers. They stayed there through the night, not sleeping, not speaking, fully awake.

Morning came with a broad brush of red on blue. When the sun was high above them they knew, without a word, that it was time to go. They got on their camels and rode slowly off towards the west, in silence, as one. They did not look back.

As before, not long after leaving, the fear came. They felt it as a single body. It twisted and turned them with its force; bending and shaking them and threatening to throw them from their camels.

Sati was calm; the fear was almost an old friend now, and his calm calmed Fellima and

Mushtina. Their breath slowed and they stopped fighting.

How long the fear lasted they did not know. They had no sense of time. All they knew was that it left as suddenly as it had come, leaving them exhausted and empty. They rode on into the west.

A little later Mushtina drew her camel up beside Sati. "Next year mother and I will come with you again," she said quietly. And Sati knew it would be so.

Sati and his family settled back into their familiar village life. And although they lived the same routines as they had before, something had changed. Everything had a new lustre, everything felt somehow more alive.

Often now, in the evening, one or two or even a small group of the villagers came to their hut to ask Sati's advice or to chat with him, or to chat of this and that with Fellima and Mushtina, or to ask for their advice, or to simply to sit in silence.

More tourists also came to the village and out for trips into the desert. Sati was able to give even more money to Meera and, in turn, Meera was able to give even more to her two other daughters. Sati even had enough money left over to give to the poorest families in the village, to ensure that they had enough food on their tables and enough clothes for their children.

Sati, Fellima and Mushtina never spoke of the flowers – not to each other nor to anyone else. They seemed somehow too tender, too delicate, to speak of.

11

One hot morning, a few years later, Meera made her slow way to Sati's door. Her voice was weak with age, but steady. She looked into his eyes with love.

"My time is short and I will soon leave this old body," she said quietly. "But I awoke last night, in the darkest hour, the threshold, knowing I have one thing to do before I leave – to come with you into the desert, to go where you go. I know not where and I know not why."

Sati looked into her eyes, a connection beyond a lifetime. "Meera, my mother, it is a hard journey and you are old," he replied.

Meera's gaze did not waver. "It is not a choice. I must come."

Sati nodded. He knew it was so. In her voice he heard the determination of her granddaughter.

In the hottest month, the time when no tourists came, Sati set off once again into the desert. This time he was accompanied by Fellima, Mushtina and Meera, as well as her two other daughters and their families. Sati needed all of his camels, which now numbered sixteen, to carry them all.

The journey was not easy. Meera needed to rest very often which slowed their progress a great deal. Eventually though they neared the heart of the desert. They fell silent. Not a word was said as the camels plodded silently over the last long stretch of sand.

Mushtina broke the quiet with a gasp. "Father," she said, pointing a few feet ahead. "Look – there are more flowers now."

Where there had been four flowers, there were now eight; small suns on the desert floor.

Sati looked over to Meera. There were tears in her eyes as he'd known there would be. Big fat joyful tears that rolled slowly down her soft wrinkled cheeks. He saw her as she had been so many years before; luminous with beauty. She looked back at him, her eyes shining – so vibrant, so alive.

Meera's three daughters helped her down from her camel. She hobbled slowly to the flowers and touched each of them gently, one by one.

"Thank you," she said quietly.

They sat down next to the flowers, in silence. They stayed there through the night, fully awake, not speaking. No time, no words, no tiredness. Then, when the sun was once again high in the sky, they stood as one and got back on their camels.

Meera looked back at the flowers as they rode off. "Goodbye," she said, and Sati heard the remembering and the longing within her voice.

And this time, a little after leaving, only the slightest shiver of fear arose in their hearts; nothing more. They hardly noticed it. As if one body they rode onwards into the west.

12

Meera died at home, in the bed she'd shared with Mushta, a week after she got back from the desert. She looked up at her family and friends crowded around her and, though she did not speak, a light shone from her eyes that said all that needed to be said as she fell into her final sleep.

Her death, as death often does, opened up a short time when people felt free to talk more personally and feel more tenderly than usual.

A steady stream of the villagers came to Sati to ask him about his trip with Meera into the desert – something that they, honouring each other's privacy as they did, would never have normally done. They'd seen the change in Meera and they wanted to know more.

Sati knew that it was, at last, time to talk to them of the flowers. He called a meeting near the well and, surrounded by all of the villagers, he told his story – from the dream that started him off on his very first journey, to finding the flower, to Mushtina's dream and his second journey, and to Meera's waking at the darkest hour and his most recent trip.

The villagers listened in silence. When Sati finished speaking a man, very old, spoke up.

"My father's father told me a tale on his knee when I was very young," he said, his voice shaking, but still echoing the hope and strength of his youth. "He told me that a very long time ago, where there is now desert, there was once a vast carpet of flowers. He said it had been like that, unchanging, for thousands of years. But then man had come along and, one by one, cut the flowers down. He told me that the flowers screamed terribly as they died, but that no one lifted a finger to help them. Then there were no more flowers. Man had made the desert barren."

The old man looked slowly around at the faces of the villagers. "It seems," he added quietly. "That my grandfather was wrong. A single flower did survive."

13

The next year in the hottest month, the time when no tourists came, Sati set off into the desert with almost the whole village in his wake. Only those villagers that were too old and too infirm to come with him stayed at home.

A great many camels were bought and borrowed from neighbouring villages and even further afield to carry everyone. It was a magnificent sight, like the old days – a great caravan of camels streaming out from the village gates, flowing towards the hidden heart of the desert.

Sati sat astride his favourite camel at the front of the caravan, his wife and daughter on their camels by his side. The way was very familiar to all three of them now and the caravan made quick progress through the emptiness of stone and sand that embraced them.

As they neared the centre of the desert the whole party fell into silence. Not a word was said as the camels plodded silently over the last long stretch of sand.

Once again it was Mushtina who broke the quiet. "Look!" she cried excitedly, pointing straight ahead. "Look! There are even more flowers now." She counted silently for a few seconds. "Sixteen of them!"

Everyone dismounted from their camels and sat next to the flowers, in silence, fully awake, through the night. And when the sun was high again in the sky they rose as one, without a word, and went back to their camels.

And this time as they rode away from the flowers no fear came, not even the slightest shiver. They rode as one body, without thinking, full and alive, into the west.

14

The village thrived and prospered as never before. In many ways it remained what it had always been, a huddle of humble huts and homes teetering on edge of the vast desert. But even more tourists came from far and wide and even more people visited from the scattered neighbouring villages.

Everyone who came was welcomed warmly. They were all treated with kindness. As a result, when they returned home they spoke enthusiastically about the village and so even more people came to visit.

The villagers were content. Although busier now with so many visitors, they spent more time talking and listening to each other, and everyone took care to ensure that all their neighbours had enough food to eat and clothes to wear.

When Sati next rode out to the flowers he was accompanied by almost all of the villagers as before, and by a small number of people from outside the village. Some of these people came from neighbouring villages and, even though the heat was stifling, some were returning tourists who had heard of the flowers when they had first come to the village.

The caravan was even more magnificent than the previous year. Longer, of course, and also more colourful and more joyous – as all those who had been to the flowers before were full of excitement about visiting them again.

This time, as Sati had known they would, they found thirty-two flowers in the heart of the desert, each as yellow as the sun.

As always, everyone sat down next to the flowers, in silence, fully awake, through the night.

When the sun was high in the sky once again the mass of people stood as one and went back to their camels and, with Sati and his family at the front, rode off into the west. There was no fear.

And when all of the people returned to their day-to-day lives they felt changed. Not always obviously, but they all felt something move, something open, and they knew that they would never be the same again.

15

Each year Sati led more and more people out into the desert. And over time, the hottest month became the busiest time in the village, with a great fair of tents and camels arriving just outside its gates. People came from all around the world, from every continent and, it seemed to Sati, from every country.

Sati's family grew too. Mushtina married and was blessed by three children, two beautiful daughters and a son. Sati loved his grandchildren with a heart that no longer knew any boundaries. He often gazed at them and his wife and his daughter and silently gave thanks for the miracle of his life.

The three children came with Sati, Fellima and Mushtina on the annual trip to the flowers. At first, when they were small, they all sat with Mushtina on a single camel, but as they grew they came to ride their own camels.

Each year Sati and his family led the growing caravan of camels and riders from the camping grounds outside the village – snaking behind them into the eternity of sand and rock. And each year the number of flowers they found doubled, covering more and more of the desert and shortening the journey from the village by minutes, then hours and then days.

And each year the people came down from their camels and sat next to flowers, in silence, fully awake, through the night. Then, when the sun was high again in the sky, they quietly got back on their camels and returned to their day-to-day lives, somehow different, somehow changed.

16

Sati became an old man; the oldest in the village. And although weaker in body than in his youth, he still led the great caravan into the desert every year, in the hottest month, his beloved Fellima and Mushtina and his grandchildren by his side.

The journey was much easier now. The flowers had overflowed riotously, wild and abundant, from the heart of the desert, doubling in numbers each year and growing in their millions on the dry sand and rock and swelling ever closer to the gates of the village. It was little more than a day's ride to reach them.

Indeed it was so easy, that visiting the flowers with Sati became more of a much-loved annual tradition than any sort of a necessity. A great many visitors didn't wait for the hottest month and the caravan anymore, but travelled to the flowers alone or in small groups, at all times of year, without any guide.

Sati often watched them as they set off into the desert. Sitting in his chair, his heart content, gazing quietly after them from the window of his small hut; the hut that he'd lived in all of his life, on the edge of the village, on the edge of the desert. The hut he'd shared with his parents. He'd never wanted any other.

His three grandchildren often visited him and found him still sitting in his chair two or three days later, by the window, smiling happily to himself as he watched the people return again to the village, somehow different, somehow changed.

Sati smiled all the time now; a smile that did not depend on the changing winds, a smile that grew out of the rich deep soil of the heart.

17

The day came as it will for us all.

As the time to visit the flowers approached, as the days became almost unbearably hot, Sati sat in his chair by the window and gazed into the desert.

He watched the endless trail of people on camels – often on his own camels as Mushtina now hired them out without a guide – setting off from the gates of the village, making the short journey to the flowers just over the horizon.

His beloved wife Fellima sat quietly by his side. They had grown old together, more and more in love; like two ancient trees whose thick-bark trunks had intertwined.

His daughter Mushtina, her husband, and their three children – Sati's grandchildren – sat on a long bench on the other side of the room.

Sati looked at them all through slow smiling eyes, full of love. He felt tired. For the first time in his life he felt truly old. His body felt heavy and weary about him. He fell asleep.

Sati gazed at the flowers, a million perfect suns. He watched them grow, one by one, filling the whole desert, growing right up to his hut.

A young man again, he rose easily from his chair and walked, full of joy, to the threshold of his door.

He looked out into the beautiful yellow flowers and paused, just for a moment, to say thank you to his family, and to say thank you for all he lived and all he had loved, and then he walked out into the flowers. He did not look back.

About the author

Neil del Strother has worked as a freelance
writer for more than 15 years. He has written for
newspapers, magazines, companies, and a range
of consultancies and government departments
working to improve the lives of children and
young people. This is his first book. Neil's
new book *The Girl with a Deer on a Lead* is
now available from www.neildelstrother.co.uk
and www.amazon.co.uk

Neil has an MA in Journalism and a DipPsych.
He is also a qualified Journey Practitioner
(www.thejourney.com) and has some experience
of shamanism, attending workshops and
taking part in healing ceremonies with the San
Bushmen in Botswana.